OGBE-DI

Knowledge is shared between people

A story written by
RAUL DOMINGUEZ

"When you get to know everything,
There is no reason to live "

CONTENTS

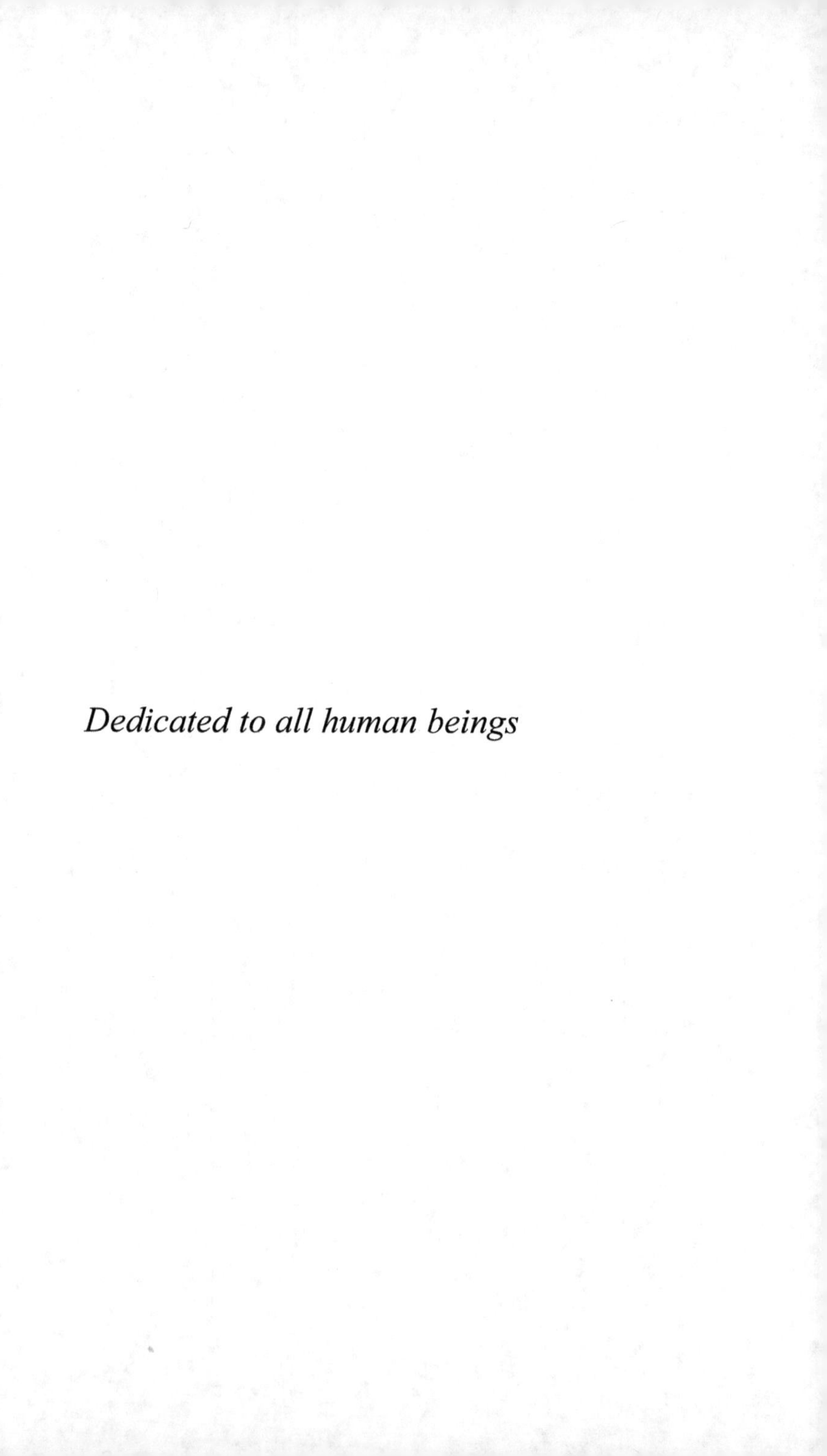

Dedicated to all human beings

CHAPTER 1
THE IYESA LAND

It was a time when the Earth was sunk in ignorance. Corruption, vice, and disinterest were those that governed in those days. There were no schools or any place where people could learn "something," so to speak, because there was not even someone to teach, and it was that nobody had anything to contribute. No one possessed any art or ability to display. Nobody knew anything.

With each passing day, the Earth was heading for destruction and collapse. People were moving towards failure. And the famine, seeing that it had high chances of success, began to haunt, little by little, the cities of the Earth.

The people beating each other, entangled in the mud of the streets, the noise and bustle of those neighborhoods, became a custom, leaving a putrid smoke smell, which came from the dead and closed places. Rotten meats of animals full of flies. Businesses no longer opened, and men walked without motivation. As if life had no meaning.

Olofi decided to do something about it to save humanity from ignorance and destruction, and create the knowledge. He put him in a man and sent him down to Earth to spread it among the people. But the man, upon reaching the Earth, disappeared. Not even Olofi in heaven could know where the knowledge was. Meanwhile, Olofi's creation was still doomed to failure.

Several years passed, and Olofi, not knowing anything about the man, decided to try one more time. In order not to fail this time, and fearing that it might be destroyed, he divided the knowledge and shared it in sixteen men that he also sent to Earth: the sixteen Olodus, apostles, chosen to change the destiny of humanity. It took several years for the last of them to reach Earth.

Olofi then selected some men to follow and serve the apostles and learn from them.

That way, knowledge could continue to spread. One of the men chosen by Olofi was Ogbe-di.

The young Ogbe-di lived in the Iyesa land and worked for Oshun, who was the queen of that place. He served as a counselor, although he was too young, according to some.

Oshun meets him the first time, at the market, while he talked about the roads, and the way he believed the time could be used.

At that time, there was only one market in those lands, Oja-Ajigbomeken. Every technology or art, or anything to trade, could be found in this market. It was several months of travel to get from some places. Rocky roads, mountains, lakes, and swampy areas were obstacles that often had to be overcome by those who needed to get there. The merchandise they bought was sometimes lost through ambushes, and the difficulties of terrain and transportation.

Ogbe-di drew routes on parchment so that each land had access to the market in less time, a project that was later carried out.

Oshun watched the boy's speech and took him as a slave to his palace to work alongside her as a counselor. Ogbe-di had to assist her in every decision-making, and she always listened to him.

It was not the worst job on Earth. And that concept of slavery was not too bad either; he was surrounded by luxuries of the palace and with the grace of the queen on his side.

He learned about love, the smile, the dance. He learned by observing, about sex, pleasure, lust, desire, and wealth. He brought his wisdom to the queen and devoted himself to thinking and understanding.

He spent hours observing the plants and smelling the Earth.

He understood the moon and its cycles, the dates and times, the crops and the cattle; All those things were the motor that drove the boy that wanted to know everything.

Oshun watched Ogbe-di every day and knew that this thin and fragile boy could go a long way if he went out to see the world more.

One afternoon she proposed to him the freedom, to know more about all the things that existed.

Ogbe-di had an inordinate thirst to know. Each word was drawn on his head, forming symbols. The course of the river, and the wind, outlined routes for him. The movement of the trees, the sound of the water, the silence; It was all a teaching, and he learned something different every day.

Oshun's offer could give him more of those things. If I had the opportunity to travel the world, I could learn more, much more. But he was not able to abandon the queen, who taught him what trust meant. Therefore, he refused and decided to continue serving her, until he have nothing to contribute to that land.

CHAPTER 2
THE PRIEST OF IYESA

The apostle Oddi-melli visited the Iyesa land. That afternoon he walked through the city and entered the taverns offering divination.

Oddi-melli was a bald man, strong, tall, seductive. Like all Olodus, he had a part of the knowledge that Olofi sent to earth and boasted about it. He was a good fortune teller. He was interpreting an oracle. He asked questions, and he received answers. His predictions were accurate. His strategy was to surprise people with the truth, and then make them believe that their problem was more significant. That way, he could ask them for more, in exchange for helping them. He was a cunning man and had many followers.

The land of Iyesa opened the doors for him, and there he settled for a time. He married a woman, whom he never showed, and he had four children.

The stories of this apostle were famous in that land, and he was talked about everywhere. He had a luxurious house, and he received many visitors every day in search of divination. His wealth grew remarkably, and one day Oshun wanted Oddi-melli to go divination for her in the palace.

At first, the Olodu, due to his arrogance, did not want to go to the palace. He believed that Oshun should see him. But he also knew that he could not miss the opportunity to attend to the Queen, so he did. He went to the palace and

Oshun received him in his private rooms. He was a little uncomfortable, he felt underrated. He hoped they would make a special reception for him, or that the Queen would offer him impressive gifts. When the palace guards guided him to where the Queen was, Ogbe-di was also there.

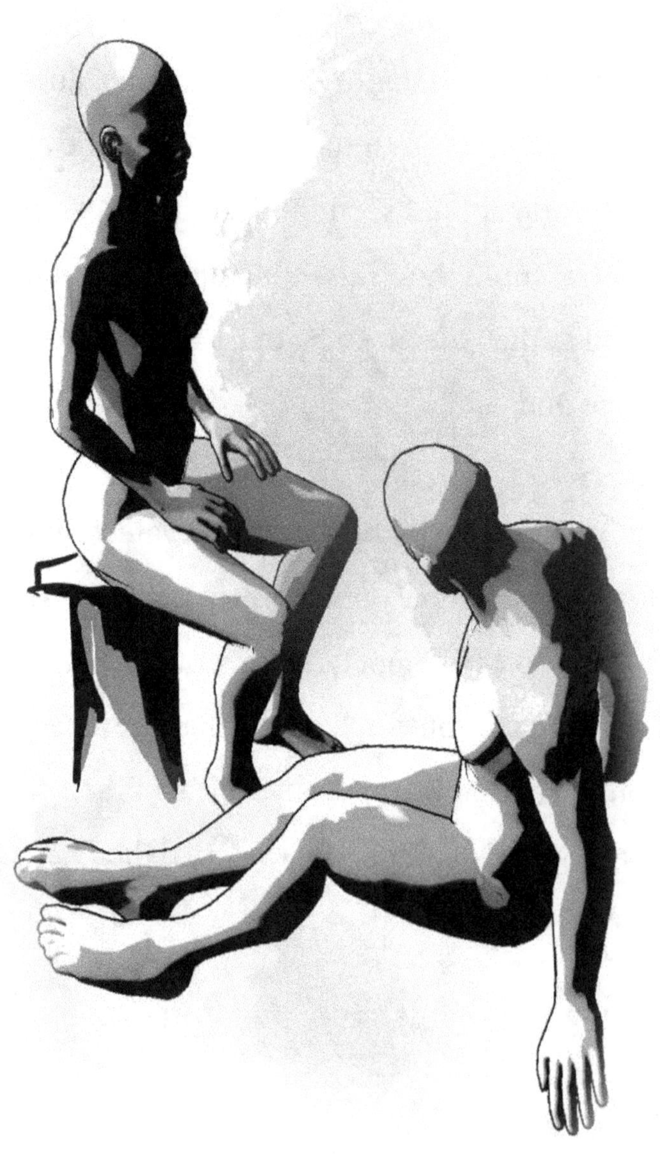

What was happening was for Ogbe-di, a new experience. He had heard that there were men who carried the knowledge by mandate of Olofi, but that was the first time that he was going to be in front of one of the Olodus.

Oddi-melli took out a mat made of dried leaves and opened it on the ground. He sat on one side with his feet outstretched and asked Oshun to sit across from him on a wooden bench. "

Ogbe-di could see that the man was following a series of steps as he progressed in divination. He also noted that Oshun was amazed at every word the Olodu uttered. The man used a divination instrument with chains and coconut rinds. The way the instrument fell to the ground after each question told

Oddi-melli what to say.

The divination was over, and Oshun was trembling from everything the man had told him. But more troubling had been the prediction that she was going to lose her sight; one day, her light would go out, and she would live in the dark if she didn't let Oddi-Melli help her. In the Queen's head, there were endless situations, which seized her once the apostle finished divination.

She did not know where to start, and she was willing to give all the riches to this man as long as he helped him. Ogbe-di approached the Queen and clasped her hands tightly. "I would like to give you some advice," he said. "May the Olodu come seven more days to make divination, and then, you can be convinced." Oshun, for the first time, since Ogbe-di was by his side, hesitated. Why should I wait? But still, he heeded the advice.

For the next seven days, Oddi-melli went to the palace to make divination for the Queen. And he followed the same patterns that Ogbe-di perceived on the first day. In addition to realizing that he always made the same movements, Ogbe-di also had a purpose with that advice he had given Oshun.

Ogbe-di didn't need to be told seven days in a row what the Queen had already heard. He needed time to learn the full secret of Oddi-Melli's divination. He would stare at the Olodu's movements and every word he said, and the ways the divination instrument fell to the ground, and he would take notes. He realized that sometimes Oddi-melli did not say what he saw in divination, to defraud the Queen.

Ogbe-di, in those seven days, was able to interpret the secret of divination. His intelligence, thirst for investigation, and learning gave him the power to grasp the teachings quickly. Oddi-melli had unknowingly been Ogbe-di's teacher.

On the seventh day, as Oddi-Melli got up from the mat, he told Oshun that he had already completed his days of divination, and the time had come to make a decision.

"What is the queen willing to offer in exchange for her salvation?" Oddi-melli said.

Ogbe-di offered Oshun an apology for

having used her. That way, he had time to learn from the Olodu, and he said to the queen that Oddi -Melli had lied to her, filling his head with ideas and situations that were not true, to obtain wealth. Oshun, uncomfortable with that situation, without doubting the words of her counselor, who had never failed her before. Also, she decides to trust Oddi-melli because he revealed truths that only she could know. She was in a severe dilemma on that occasion. Oddi-melli was amazed at Ogbe-di's discovery, and although what he spoke was right, he never acknowledged his deception to the queen.

Oddi-melli was a soothsayer; he was one of the sixteen Olodus to whom Olofi had entrusted part of the knowledge; He had the power of divination and wisdom, and he showed his potential. Amidst all the tension, Oddi-melli described to Oshun what she kept in a trunk in her room; He also told her how many stones the palace had been built with, how much wealth she possessed, the name of the man the queen loved, and that man was not her husband. That and other truths made Oshun feel threatened and tipped the scales in Oddi-Melli's favor, and ordered Ogbe-di taken prisoner.

Oshun didn't like the decision, but it was what he had to do under the circumstances. If this man revealed the queen's secrets, her husband could kill her.

Ogbe-di was also not comfortable with Oshun's determination and, in the struggle with the guards, raised his voice and said:

"I also have the power of divination, my queen. If you allow me, with the same Oddi-melli instruments, I could tell you what his movements are going to be in the coming days".

Everyone was amazed at Ogbe-di's words. Even one of the guards scoffed at what he had said. Oshun thought each statement from his adviser had been accurate up to that point. On the other hand, if what he said was true, she might know if Oddi-melli tells the secrets.

"Yes, I accept," Oshun replied. "You will read Oddi-Melli's oracle for him. And we will check if what you say is true. If you lie, you will die".

Ogbe-di spread the mat on the floor and sat down in the same position Oddi-melli had. He flawlessly executed each of the rituals that the Olodu performed during those seven days, he pronounced the prayers and made the divination.

Ogbe-di memorized everything he read in the oracle, and, when he finished, he told the queen that he would say to her, only her, every sunrise, what would happen that day. That was the way he had to protect himself from death and regain Oshun's confidence.

They led him to a cell; Prisoner of his thirst and ambition to learn, in a cold and humid room, at the top of the palace. No windows, no bed to rest. With only the sunlight, which was passing through a hole, which was in one of the walls. Darkness gripped the entire cell. It was difficult for him to see his hands.

That night he could not sleep because of the noise of the rats, and the fear of the dark solitude that he was living. And he received no food until dawn.

That was the first day, in a long time, that the land of Iyesa did not use the advice of Ogbe-di.

One of the villages, several months ago, had had problems with the fertility of its soils, and its crops were damaged. There only lived children, women, and the elderly, who were wandering from another land where their homes had been looted, and the men who went out to fight, were killed. They lived off the few provisions that remained, and if something were not done about it, the inhabitants of that town would eventually starve to death.

The sun penetrated through the crack in

the wall of the cold cell, and it was the first day.

Oshun woke up early and eager to hear Ogbe-di's first divination, while everyone in the palace looked everywhere for the queen's ivory comb.

Combing the Oshun's long and curly hair was a ritual every morning. Her five ladies-in-waiting devoted all their efforts to embellishing her since the first ray of daylight came out every day. That morning, the comb did not appear. She tied her hair up with knitting needles, and the ladies put on her brightest dresses. Although she was not pleased, she was in a hurry to know what Ogbe-di had to say to her, and she did not want to waste any more time searching for the comb.

Ogbe-di heard the latch on the thick door of the dark cell, and when it opened, Oshun entered. In her hands, she carried a plate with some leftovers, pieces of coconut and wine for the prisoner to feed on, while the guard waited outside the cell.

"I'm waiting for the divination," Oshun said, holding the plate and threatening not to give it to her until she got what she wanted. With sadness and disappointment reflected on his face, the young Ogbe-di rose from the ground and, adjusting his dirty clothes, said to her:

"The Olodu will not tell your secrets today, my queen. He will go to the mountain to look for herbs, and he will be preparing the powder for the rest of the day in his house".

Oshun appointed two guards to follow Oddi-melli and watch his house, to verify that what Ogbe-di said was true.

That day was very long for the palace guards. They also discovered that all the fruits of the real trees had disappeared, and they spent all their time investigating who had stolen them.

Oddi-melli was at his house that morning attending to the guests who were seeking divination, and then he went off to the bush to look for the herbs. When he returned, he was sacrificing animals and preparing witchcraft.

Ogbe-di's prediction was accurate. Oshun stared at him with amazement and respect, also with regret for the injustice she was committing. She brought him trays of food and wine and locked him up again.

Ogbe-di took advantage of the low light and wrote a lot on the walls of his cell. He wrote stories and thoughts, drew figures, and meditated to find peace of mind. He did not take a bite of the food that was brought to him, nor did he sleep. He only drank the water that sweated the rocks on the walls of the palace.

At nightfall, and after dinner, Oshun and her husband Ogun went to their rooms and, after talking for several hours, fell asleep. In the middle of the night, Ogun quietly got up and left the room, unaware that Oshun had heard him. Without moving, she opened her eyes and felt her husband leave.

The queen remained in the window watching if the husband left the palace, and she implored Olofi that this should not happen. She watched Ogun walk away, cautious, and after so much thinking, the dream overcame her.

The next morning, Ogun was already there.

The second dawn came as well, and the queen went to receive the divination that she had for her that second day.

Oddi-melli will come to the palace, my queen. He will be restless and doubtful, and he will want to know if I was right. "

Oshun left the cell and yanked the door closed. What Ogbe-di was saying was happening, but she knew nothing about Oddi-melli's intentions with the secrets he knew about her.

The queen's concern did not let her think. That morning she also couldn't comb her hair.

Several hours passed, and Ogbe-di, with the coconut crusts of the first day, built pieces similar to those that Oddi-melli used to guess, and he prayed and consecrated them.

Meanwhile, the Olodu Oddi-melli was arriving at the palace gate, just as Ogbe-di had predicted. He met with Oshun, and they talked about many things. Oshun confessed to her that, due to all the confusion, she was not convinced that she wanted him to help her. She preferred to pass the time and see another Olodu, in another land.

Oddly, the queen poured the powder into her wine glass and waited for Oshun to drink it. Minutes after she told him that Ogbe-di had been unable to guess anything, he left satisfied and let the spell take effect on Oshun.

Ogbe-di made divination for himself all that afternoon. He gathered up the leftovers from the food and wiped them away with the ray of sunlight streaming through the crack in the wall. He spent all day chasing the sun around the cell to dry all the ingredients. At night he covered them in his black robe and devoted himself to meditation. He neither slept nor ate.

Ogun went out again at night while Oshun slept. She saw him again, from his window, as he was walking away from the palace.

She was preparing to call a guard to send him on, but at that moment, there was a wail that echoed in the walls of the palace. Like someone crying. The silence of the night helped the echo of that voice become increasingly chilling and reach every corner of Oshun's palace.

The guards and the queen, in the middle of the night, chased the echo of that voice, while they lit with torches. The wail grew louder each time they approached the main room and then disappeared. When they went away, it was heard again. It was a mystery that kept them that way for a while until the sound was utterly lost in the silence.

The voice was not heard back, and Oshun returned to his room. Ogun must be away already. There was no use chasing him. They had wasted a lot of time searching for the source of the lament.

The third day came earlier than usual. And, before sunrise, shouts that broke Ogbe-di's concentration was already heard in the hallways of the palace. He opened his eyes and breathed.

"The queen cannot see," they shouted. "Oshun has gone blind." He, more worried than surprised, opened the robe that wrapped the ingredients, and with a stone, he began to crush them all. He made a powder of them. He got up from the floor, fixed his clothes, and took all the dust in his hands. He clenched his fists and stood in front of the door. When they opened, two women were leading Oshun before him. The queen's handsome face was still the most beautiful he had ever seen. But her eyes were colorless. There was a gray in her gaze that was lost through him.

"How could you not guess this?" She asked. Before he said another word, the young Ogbe-di blew the dust on his face, and the lost and gray gaze of the beautiful queen was as before. She regained her sight, and when she looked up, the low light that entered allowed her to see clearly all the writings in the cell. Oshun approached the walls and was reading every prophecy that Ogbe-di had left there. Thus she discovered that the ivory comb had been stolen by one of the guards, commissioned by Oddi-melli, to use her hair in the dust to blind her. The one who had stolen his fruits from the royal trees had been Ogun, who did it several nights, while he believed that the queen slept, to take them to the people of a village who were starving because they lost their crops.

The voice heard in the silence of the night in the palace was from one of Oshun's maids, who realized that the queen had discovered her husband, and did it to mislead her and make her desist from sending him to follow.

The ingredients of the powder that left her blind were also written on the walls, and the way Oddi-melli gave it to her in the wine.

The queen could taste her tears. Everything was written on those walls.

Ogbe-di knew everything that was happening, and Oshun felt rage despite being cured by blindness and showing that he was also a fortune teller. Anger seized her because Ogbe-di had not told her the truth and allowed her to be set up and left in total darkness.

"The truth is I told you, my queen. And you must be blind for Oddi-melli's divination to be fulfilled," Ogbe-di told the queen. "But also, I needed to show him that salvation did not come from Oddi-melli's hand. It was a misfortune that he would bring, and he was trying to enrich himself with it."

Oshun was still crying because she couldn't accept what was happening to her. Ogbe-di told him that Oddi-melli was never going to tell the secrets. That there was no evidence to take any action against Olodu. Oshun did not hesitate to listen to Ogbe-di and gave him his freedom.

Ogbe-di continued to live in the palace, and Oshun ordered to build him a temple where he would serve as a priest.

The Awo Ogbe-di's works and predictions were astonishing. In addition to helping people, he also received the grace of healings. He knew plants, learned about sorcery, and was Oshun's fortune teller after that. The inhabitants of the Iyesa land visited him for divination and to bring him offerings. The rumor soon spread that Oddi-melli had wanted to defraud the queen.

Ogbe-di, attracted by knowledge and the ambition to learn, went into the mountains for seven days, to understand the darkness and silence. He wanted to know the birds and the shadows. He visited the caves of the men who had previously been there.

He returned to the Iyesa land and continued guessing and helping people. He practiced black magic and learned from the spirits of the men who had died. His power grew inordinately every minute, and his stories reached Olofi's ears in the sky.

In his fortune-telling days, he met a woman. She was not a beautiful woman with a face, her face was long and blotchy as if she was losing skin color, but her body was impressive. That woman's protruding curves drove Ogbe-di mad. She was always covered by a cloth that only revealed her eyes. She visited him several times, and each time he was amazed by the woman's stunning body and did not pay attention to the stains on his face. She felt good every time she removed the cloth before Ogbe-di because it didn't make her feel like a monster, and he ignored her flaws.

They met several times and started a romance. She was married and had children. The love between them became very strong, and they often encountered on the outskirts of the city.

Ogbe-di kept waiting on several occasions, and she did not come to the meeting because she could not get rid of her husband. Thus the months passed, and it was increasingly difficult to see each other. Their dates were complicated, and their forbidden idyll dragged them into madness and despair. Prejudice and his dedication as a priest in the Iyesa land would never allow him to be happy next to the woman he loved.

It was custom at that time when someone died, and the corpse was offered to the gods; It was carried at the foot of a tree so that the body fertilized the earth and served as food for the animals.

That sacrifice would buy the forgiveness of the soul to be able to reach the foot of Olofi.

Ogbe-di prepared witchcraft for her beloved to take and be presumed dead. Once they left her on the tree, he would wake her up, and they could escape together from Iyesa.

That night the woman kissed her children and took the spell. The next morning, they were all mourning the loss.

The husband did not want the details to be released, because it could bring him a bad reputation that his wife had died in strange circumstances. He decided to take the corpse alone to the tree of the gods.

Hidden in the bushes, Ogbe-di kept watch all the time, and when they were left alone, he woke her up from the spell. So far, they were following a plan, but after they passed the mountains that marked the limits of that land, they did not know where to go. The woman had left her life behind to follow Ogbe-di and bet on love. And he gave up the luxuries of the palace and all his followers, ready to build a new life with that woman who hypnotized him.

In this way, they left the domain of Queen Oshun behind, and Ogbe-di marched with his wife to other lands, without knowing what their destiny would be. At least not yet.

CHAPTER 3
THE FIRST BURIAL

A few months passed before the absence of Ogbe-di was felt in Iyesa. Primarily since they were used to him disappearing in search of knowledge. But this time, it had been a long time.

Ogbe-di and her lover were living in the mountains, where they could enjoy their love without being disturbed. He gave up knowledge and service to others in exchange for spending his happy days with his lover.

A fair was held in Oja-Ajigbomeken, where all the lands were going to show their technologies and products could be purchased at an excellent price. Sales those days would be outstanding.

Oddi-melli sent his eldest son to that distant region to search the market for seeds that he could not find in Iyesa, and that he needed for his rites and witchcraft. Now that Ogbe-di was lost, he had gained a following again.

The boy searched the market for the seeds his father had ordered, but far from that, he was sure that he had seen his mother selling fruits there. He hid in the crowd and observed.

There was what appeared to be his mother with a wooden cart. The huge wheels didn't let the boy make sure it was her. As she approached cautiously among the people, she could perceive her bare face, with the same spots that made her look as if she was losing her skin color.

Dumbfounded, the boy did not know what to do at the time. His mother had died months ago, or so he believed. He ran out of the market for getting the seeds that his father ordered, and after several weeks he came home.

He quickly told Oddi-melli that he had

seen his mother at the market, and that was why he had forgotten the seeds. The father struck him and punished him in the sun for insulting his mother's memory. So Oddi-Melli sent another of the sons to the market in search of the seeds.

Ogbe-di and his beloved lived in the mountains near Oja-Ajigbomeken. They had grown fruit and sold their products every morning in the market. The era of palace luxury was over for Ogbe-di, who had decided to give up everything for love.

It didn't take long for Oddi-Melli's other son to arrive at the market, and, like the oldest of the four, he was also petrified to see his mother.

The brother had already said it, but still, he had not believed him. He had seen his dead mother being brought before the gods. He decided to stay awhile to follow her, but the woman only sold her crops all day.

Then, in the evening, the woman left with her cart, and the boy did not dare to approach. He left for Iyesa, and when he got home, hardly breathing, he told his father what he had seen.

Oddi-melli, already alarmed, began to suspect. Still, she punished the boy in the yard, in the sun, for not bringing him the seeds he had ordered.

He sent another of his sons to corroborate the story and also return with his seeds. The boy left the next morning. Upon arrival, several weeks later, he searched all over Oja-Ajigbomeken, but could not find his mother. He decided to stay there in the hope of finding her. The desire to see her again made him spend several days hanging around the market.

The morning he decided to leave, with the seeds of his father, and convinced that it had been a prank by his brothers, walking away, on the way to the market, in his wagon, he saw his mother passed away, vanished in the morning mist, and the boy, drowning in despair, shouted his name. He stared at her in the solid fog, and although he was too fast to be sure, the woman, hearing her name, turned to look.

The third of the children going to his house and told his father that he had also seen his mother at the market.

Oddi-melli decided to check for himself the history of his children and set out for Oja-Ajigbomeken.

He was walking through the market for several hours before seeing her. But there she was. She was laughing among women, with baskets full of fruit, proclaiming the sale. Oddi-melli stood still, motionless, stunned.

A ringing in his ears left him for a long time without listening, watching his wife move happily, while the walkers stumbled over him. Memories assailed him of when he met her, how he bore her four children, and when he found her dead that day. He knew that she had cheated on him.

That woman had been able to abandon him and her children, and she still didn't understand why she had done it. That is not the woman he met and married. But that was her, his wife, the mother of his children, who had died.

The woman, in turn, extinguished her smile when she saw her husband in front of her, looking at her with red eyes and lit with fire, demanding revenge. She released the fruits and ran away, nor did she know where she was going. He hurried after her as she stumbled in his wake, unstable because she kept looking back to make sure she kept a reasonable distance from the man who was not looking at her with good intentions.

She was running, but she was getting more and more nervous, and the more nervous she got, the heavier her step became, and she stumbled over the boxes and people.

He walked safe, agile; He had no idea what was going to do, but all knew was that he had to get to where she was. In his path he threw the things he found, and shoved people away, and everything that stood between him and that ungrateful and treacherous woman.

As he passed the fishmonger's shop, he grabbed a knife and pounced on the woman. He stabbed her thirty-seven times, and she was still alive. The market people fled upon seeing such an outrage.

Oddi-melli stared at his wife as her life drained away. She breathed her last breath, and he stayed there until he made sure she was dead this time. With the uproar in the market, Ogbe-di was guided by curiosity, and when he was close, he could see that it was his beloved who was lying dead in her husband's arms. His instincts urged him to come to her defense, but she no longer lived.

And a heroic act could lead him to death too. It left the market. Scared, and walked all day. And in his constant wandering, he found a fat man, with very dark and shiny skin. This man was dressed in white, with bands of colored fabrics hanging from his waist. As he passed him by, the lord sounded some bells hanging from his bracelet. The sound of the jingle made Ogbe-di turn.

"Osalo-Fobello," said the man and bowed. "You're not going to rest until you see her again, are you?" He asked.

"He could be here until my death," replied Ogbe-di.

"If I let you see her one last time, will you go away?" Osalo-Fobello asked again.

"Why would you do it? You don't even know me," Ogbe-di said intrigued and, drowning in his grief, turned his back on him and continued walking with his head down. He failed to take three steps and saw his wife's feet before him. He looked up, and there she was.

They stared at each other for a few seconds, and without being able to say a word, she turned to see the man who allowed her to say goodbye to her beloved, in a gesture of thanks and with her eyes flooded with tears. When the sight returned, she was no longer there.

"I am a fortune-teller, like you. And a sorcerer. You must continue on your way. Someday you are going to have the opportunity to meet whom no one can see in life, and I need you to tell her about me". Ogbe-di heard the man say while searching insistently for the ghost of the woman, who had already disappeared, just like Osalo-Fobello.

Still blinded by the woman's embarrassment and betrayal, the husband decided to divide her body into four pieces, so that there was no possibility that it would appear again, and buried each of the parts in different places around Oja -Ajigbomeken.

Oddi-melli left the market and has never been heard from in the Iyesa land ever since.

He, with his children, disappeared without a trace.

That was the first burial ever made on earth. And it was a woman.

CHAPTER 4
THE SECRETARY OF ORUNMILA

gbe-di returned to the temple shortly after the death of her beloved, and spent several days without receiving visitors, until Oshun, seeing that the man was no longer the same, she offered him a job. Eager to help him, she entrusted him to go to Ife land, to work for Orunmila. He hesitated for a moment, but the days without his beloved seemed small, and everything forced him to remember.

Orunmila was a significant priest in the land of Ife. A wise man who had a secretary named Ogbe-sa.

Ogbe-sa had, among his duties, that of being in charge of waking Orunmila every morning with a prayer. But as time went on, he got comfortable and gained confidence in Orunmila's house. He no longer did his job the same way as before. Sometimes he would touch him to wake him up, or he would just pick him up in the sunlight.

That made Orunmila not wake up in a good mood and took it out on his wife, who began to get uncomfortable with Ogbe-sa's work. Speaking to Oshun, one afternoon at the market, Yeye Matero told the queen of her misfortune and told her of her eagerness to get a new secretary for her husband and thus fire Ogbe-sa and hire someone who could wake up Orunmila the right way. That was how Ogbe-di went to Ife land. Yeye Matero taught her the prayer to wake Orunmila and made sure that Ogbe-sa was not in the house that morning. Ogbe-di performed the invocation and woke up the priest. Orunmila started her day with a perfect attitude and did not even realize that Ogbe-di was now her secretary.

With his extraordinary intelligence and incredible ability for learning, Ogbe-di spent hours studying the priest's books; Books that revealed the secret of how to invoke the knowledge of the sixteen Olodus and use it in divination. Ogbe-di believed that if he learned his secret, he could have all the knowledge, and his wisdom grew.

But he realized that he always needed to summon the Olodus to guess. He would never know everything. He remained in the priest's service for three years, and there came a time when, whenever Orunmila asked him something, he already knew the answer. No place or thing he looked at made him wonder anything, did not arouse curiosity in him. He had realized that this place had nothing more to offer him. One morning Orunmila had to wake up alone. Ogbe-di was gone.

CHAPTER 5
THE MAN IN THE RED HAT

He wandered along the path that led away from that town, to a crossroads. There he stopped for several hours deciding which direction to go. And he advanced, safe and straight, towards the land of Adifa. He had some money, and he stayed in a tavern. There he locked himself in his room for days on end with his nights without leaving. The people of that city had already heard of that hermit who did not show himself. In the tavern, he met a man who sat at the end of the hall every evening in a place without light. The man asked for fish soup and sat in the same seat for hours until he left. He acted as if he expected something that would come at some point. But the rush was not noticeable to him either. The intrigue and mystery of this man brought Ogbe-di out of his room. He began to prowl the tavern to find out what was the secret that the lord was hiding.

After several nights spying on him, Ogbe-di approached him and offered him a glass of wine.

The lord wore a red hat and miserable clothes, but he was not poor; Ogbe-di was able to notice by particular objects hanging from the rope that tied his waist—piercing gaze and a thick white beard. So white. The hands were not wrinkled, that also amazed Ogbe-di, and caused him even more interest, to discover all the enigma that contained the silence of the man in the red hat.

He was in front of that older man for several nights, asking him questions, but he was only watching him. Ogbe-di believed for a moment that he couldn't speak.

People in the tavern looked at them strangely. It was rare for someone to approach this man. And even less could they imagine that whoever did it was the hermit of the town, of whom nobody knew anything; Two weird madmen. That was them for the rest.

Ogbe-di asked him many questions, but the man did not answer any. It was when Ogbe-di told him his name that he reacted. The expression on his tired face, which expressed nothing, had reflected hope. As if what seemed to be waiting depended on that name.

"Ogbe-di, the priest of Iyesa?" Replied the man. Amazed, Ogbe-di, had the impression that this man knew him. Perhaps his exploits from the land of Oshun had traveled the cities, and he was famous. That would have been a good reason. The significant fact is that he had managed to make this man break the silence.

The man in the red hat was 365 years old and had been sent to earth long before the

Olodus, with all knowledge. With the enormous weight of knowledge on his head. He was wandering all those years and always tried to do what Olofi told him to do, distribute knowledge among men. The task was too high for him alone, and he felt that his effort was in vain. He delivered knowledge to people, then those people to others. Some made good use of it, but others profited, and some selfish took it until his death, and that knowledge was lost. And again, knowledge returned to him, with the eternal purpose of distributing it again. While delivering something, another portion was returned to him. And he never finished his commission.

At 365 years old, that man all he wanted was to die. His dedication to offering knowledge faded, and he stopped trying. To him, humans were not worthy of knowledge.

The older man told him that, through divination, he knew that he would have to wait in that tavern until someone came to whom he would give all his wisdom, to be able to rest forever from that heavy burden. He also commented that he had heard the men talk about Ogbe-di, the priest of Iyesa; That he was thirsty to learn everything. In this way, he continued his routine of going to the tavern and having his soup. Retire to sleep.

The next day he walked through the streets of Adifa to the bar, and so on until he finally heard his name from his lips. And he understood everything; it was him. The man who had waited so many years. The man who wanted to know everything.

He did not deceive him, he told the whole truth to Ogbe-di. He, ready to receive the power of knowledge, blind with the desire to know what were the mysteries that the earth was hiding, prepared to march next to the man in the hat red and absorb all its wisdom; All the knowledge that the gods gave him; All the knowledge in the world. As the older man's wisdom nourished him, he felt that he grew. His size was physically the same, but he perceived himself above the trees, with a force of spirit and greatness.

The older man, for his part, each time he detached himself from a knowledge potion, the years he had were more noticeable. The hands began to weaken, and the bones in the legs were already prominent. The face, through the beard, was gaining wrinkles and black spots, warts, calluses. That man's bright gaze was disappearing and became opaque, with clouds in his eyes, which prevented him from seeing well. The beard was no longer white; it was gray. He lost some nails and had to stop several times to rest. Ogbe-di searched for him for food and carried him on his back for hours. The man in the red hat had shrunk in size; he was hunched over. His voice was no longer firm. Sometimes he would look up, waiting for the words to come. His memory failed him, but his eagerness to rest was unsurpassed. The flabby skin began to tear. A rib bone broke as Ogbe-di carried it. They had to stay several days in a shelter because they could not advance any further. Still, from his pain, she remained to teach him. The hat was no longer on his head. It covered his eyes. He had lost all his hair and had to tie the clothes tighter around his waist. His voice weighed on him, and he couldn't see anything anymore. He spoke regularly, determined to deliver every last drop of his knowledge to Ogbe-di, who had to approach to listen to him.

The feeling of satisfaction flooded the older man after he had delivered the heavy burden of knowledge. There was a smile on his face while he seemed to be observing something with his blind gaze. He could see something that, even with all the knowledge, Ogbe-di could not understand.

That man's life was extinguished that day. And Ogbe-di had become the wisest man on earth. He knew everything, he knew about destiny, about red roses, knew about science, about agriculture, he knew about taste and emotions. He knew about laughter, business, evolution. He knew about life. Yes, he knew about the cycle of life. Ogbe-di had no questions. He knew everything.

The feeling of peace could be transmitted through the still-hot corpse of the man in the red hat. And in those last few minutes Ogbe-di also knew what was happening. The motor of the older man's body had stopped, and his time was up. The scientific and religious version of why a person dies, and how also re-emerged in Ogbe-di's thinking, and it happened; the last breath. The older man took a deep breath and, in a lament, expelled him, enveloping the soul and gently releasing it from himself. The man's body, without his red hat, lay on the wet grass, and the soul was gone. "But ... where to?" Towards death, of course. "But ... what is death? What is there?" Ogbe-di was stunned and inert in an instant. A question that the man who knew everything couldn't answer. He searched within himself, and no matter how hard he tried, he didn't have the answer. He was the wisest man on earth, but now he was convinced that he didn't know everything.

CHAPTER 6
THE MISSION OF OGBE-DI

Ogbe-di buried the man in the middle of the forest, in the shade of lush old trees, with the sound of birds and the fall of water from a waterfall. It was an excellent place to rest. He remained several days there, looking at that red hat on top of the older man's grave, trying to understand where he had gone. He felt small again.

Maybe the older man couldn't teach him

everything? He needed to clarify his doubts. He did not feel that he possessed all the knowledge because he had a doubt.

Seeing that there was no answer, he left the forest and returned to Adifa.

Ogbe-di made various divinations and gained many followers. Over time he built a large house, and he had many servants. And his stories were heard throughout the length and breadth of the earth. The apostles tried to avoid the land of Adifa, fearing the wisdom of Ogbe-di. They felt threatened because they already knew that there was a man who had all the knowledge. The same knowledge that had been divided between them.

A single man who had the power of the sixteen Olodus and knowledge is power. He was the most powerful man on earth, and they made him king of Adifa.

Olofi could not allow a wiser man than the Olodus and decided to end the days of Ogbe-di. When he was before him, he questioned him, trying to understand how he had obtained the knowledge, and he told him about the older man; From the years he had lived, from Olofi's charge and how he saw him die.

Ogbe-di answered every question Olofi asked him until he got tired and accepted that he was the wisest man in the world; Still, he was convinced that he must die. Several deities intervened in Ogbe-di's favor, but it was useless. Olofi was sure that a single man should not possess all the knowledge. He had already failed once.

Ogbe-di, with his wise prose, convinced Olofi to let him live; meanwhile, he would strive to distribute knowledge among men, and once he had delivered everything, he could take it from the earth.

Ogbe-di began preparing speeches to convey everything he knew to the people. I did not want to fail; it happened to him as the man in the red hat, and he lost consciousness. He wanted to make sure that it would reach many people and that they distribute it in turn.

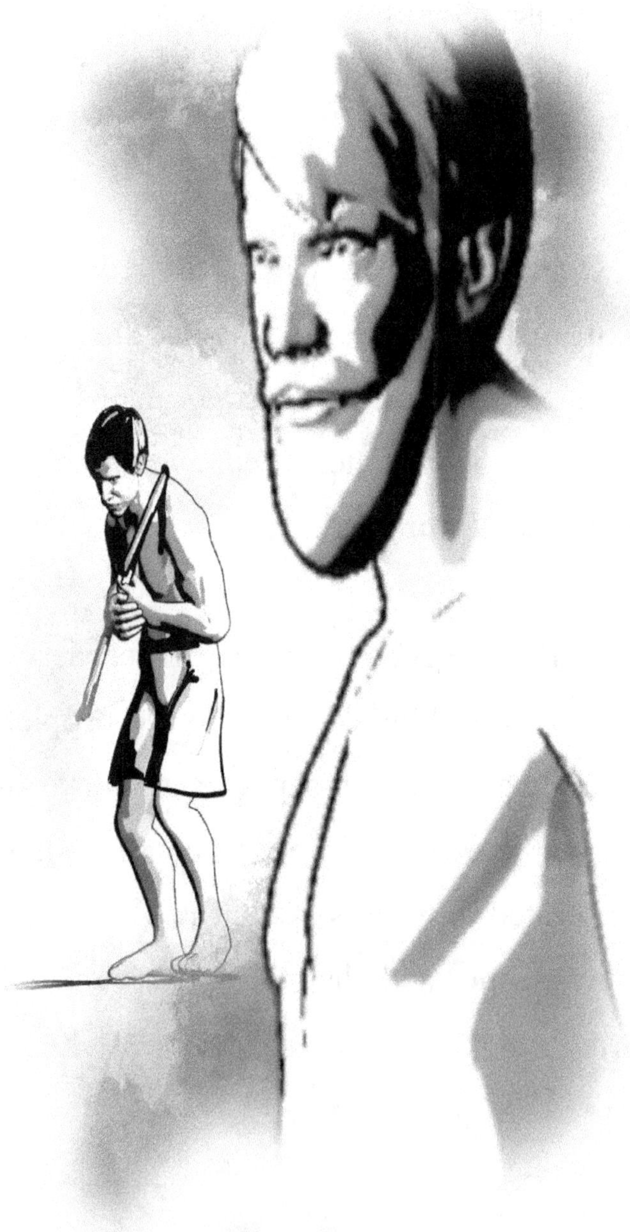

Olofi sent Elegua to follow Ogbe-di to make sure he was doing his job well and to determine when he would be ready to leave the land.

Ogbe-di left the land of Adifa once he made sure that he had distributed a portion of knowledge about the inhabitants of the city. He marched aimlessly, but surely because he knew where he had to go. In the next town, he came to he bought cattle and had followers, and his fortune grew. He had a large farm and servants.

Elegua followed closely. Every day, Elegua disguised himself as someone different so as not to be discovered by Ogbe-di. He participated in each of his speeches. The teachings of the sage Ogbe-di were interesting. But he always suspected: how a single man could possess all the knowledge?

In each of Ogbe-di's presentations, Elegua asked him a question to check his abilities. And every time Ogbe-di had the answer. Elegua wondered every day what the reason that motivated Ogbe-di to live was.

Once you know everything, life loses meaning. You stop wanting to know because there is nothing to learn. You stop looking because there is nothing to find. You know what will happen to the next second and what tomorrow will be like. You control destiny by knowing everything.

Why does Ogbe-di keep fighting and advancing? I should have lost the enthusiasm and the will to live. But, instead, he continued on his way to something he was sure he would find from his determination. But what was it? That is what intrigued Elegua. What was the reason that drove Ogbe-di to move on? Was there something I didn't know? Elegua knew that Ogbe-di was the wisest man on earth, but he was sure that he did not know everything; Something was missing to discover that it gave him reasons to continue living.

Ogbe-di came to control the roads and became the owner of a river through which they transported food between the cities. They made a sculpture in one of the towns where he was. He had two women as he passed through the lands; they had children. His mission did not allow him to stay long in the same place. He continued alone through the land, offering everyone the knowledge. And Elegua insisted on asking him something that he already knew.

Ogbe-di was careful. He was clear that he had to buy time so that Olofi would not take it away. So he never told all the things he knew. If he talked about trees, he always left a little secret that he would not share. That way, when Olofi called him, he could tell him that there was a lack of knowledge to pass out. So he thought.

Elegua was already tired of following Ogbe-di around the world. He wanted to have fun and do other things. He was tied to that man's destiny. He then decided to tell Olofi that he already believed that Ogbe-di had completed his mission on earth, and Ogbe-di received the call.

The people on earth implored the heavens to let them enjoy Ogbe-di's wisdom for a while longer. That his knowledge was enriching on earth, and they still believed that they could learn more from him. Olofi decided to give Ogbe-di an extension and sent Elegua again to follow in his footsteps.

CHAPTER 7
THE CURSE OF AGANA ERI

he next land that Ogbe-di visited was mixed with the sea. An impressive city, where the houses were built on bridges, and some rocks separated the coasts from the land; A thriving place whose crops were the best seen. Mountains rose, and the trees were vast and leafy. The wind that blew caressed your face and made you feel like you were talking.

Pumpkins and watermelons grew as big as carriages, and the fruits of the trees watered on the ground.

The owner of that land was called Orichaoko. A simple man, dedicated to his crops and the progress of his nation. He always passed the roads with his cart pushed by two sturdy oxen that looked bright from the sun's reflection on the skins.

Every day the land was invaded by the sea. The houses were located high, so there was no flooding. The sea traveled the roads and, after a few hours, returned to its level. People, in times of high tide, navigated the streets.

Upon arrival, Ogbe-di immediately began to share his wisdom and brought together the wealthiest people in that land to teach them how they could stop the floods.

Agana Eri, one of Olofi's wives on earth, also lived there. The sailors arrived at the ports of that place dragged by the enveloping song of Agana Eri. No one could see her, at least not entirely. She was a sorceress who had her home in a cave deep in the sea and had never set foot on the land. He only let her beautiful face see through the crystalline waters of the coasts.

Orichaoko met the beautiful woman who attracted outsiders to negotiate on their land and wanted to thank him. The beautiful woman brought her head to the surface and smiled at Orichaoko. The woman's piercing and captivating gaze piqued his interest, and her spells and magnetism caught him. The next day he got closer and the next day even more. And he was able to talk to the woman once, and then again until they fell in love without touching, without kissing.

Agana Eri was not just the beautiful face Orichaoko had seen. She had one leg more full than the other and was missing a breast. She had balls in her stomach, and that had made her hide from people in the dark depth of the sea. She felt the need to tell Orichaoko of her significant defect if she wanted to progress in the relationship, and he, blind with love, did not hesitate a minute to ask Olofi for permission to marry one of his wives on earth.

Seeing the sincere love that they professed each other, Olofi agreed to the request under the promise of Orichaoko, never to mention the woman's defect, and that thus, she did not have to go through the embarrassment.

Agana Eri, full of complexes, made dresses that covered her body so that no one on earth knew her secret, and she went to live with Orichaoko.

Ogbe-di continued to insist on building canals to protect the city from floods. And he also taught men new methods of storing water in times of drought. He tried, in turn, to connect with death to find the answer to the only thing he did not know; He brought to that land the secret of spiritualism and spread witchcraft and occultism.

Meanwhile, Elegua kept a close watch on him, disguising himself and hiding to discover what was the mystery of Ogbe-di. There was still a lot of wisdom left for Ogbe-di, who was still cautious, avoiding sharing it all so that there would always be something to claim Olofi if he wanted to take it back to him, but there was not much left to teach, and he had to continue showing his wisdom to buy time. He repeated the speeches and explained the same thing several times. And Elegua was beginning to notice it.

In addition to tilling the land, Orichaoko had a funeral business. It was the custom of their ancestors to cover the body of the deceased with cloth, put two coins in their eyes and pray to the gods of death for a whole night, to collect that soul and guide it until its eternal rest. Then they buried the body in the ground.

Ogbe-di heard about Orichaoko's hobbies and decided to meet him. One morning, in the port. While Orichaoko was selling vegetables to some sailors, Ogbe-di approached him to speak to him. Orichaoko was someone of few words, introverted and distrustful, and Ogbe-di knew that just by observing him, as she walked towards him. Therefore, she decided to seduce him by offering him a gift. A large umbrella made entirely of wooden slats and carved with incredible art. Orichaoko could not accept that gift. But of course, Ogbe-di also knew that. So he gave it to him in exchange for allowing him to carefully investigate his graves and the bodies of the dead for investigation.

Elegua disguised himself as a young man, homeless and hungry, and approached Ogbe-di to follow him even more closely. He was hoping that he would hire him as his assistant and thus know what he was writing down in his notebooks; what Ogbe-di was investigating, to decipher the enigma that kept him uneasy.

On one of the trips to the Orichaoko fields, Elegua approached Ogbe-di and asked for his job. At first, he didn't want to give it to him, but after a while, he looked at the boy and hired him. He was filled with grief and a desire to help, and he also needed someone to assist him in his work.

Ogbe-di built a temple in that city next to a leafy ceiba tree, on top of a mountain. He gave speeches and had scheduled at different times of the day when he received groups of people to provide them with more of his wisdom; More of that knowledge that was already running out. Meanwhile, he was analyzing the dead bodies of the men. He unearthed some corpse to observe it is interior and had it for several hours, days until the stench forced him to dispose of it. He realized that the body was not going to teach him anything. Once the soul left it, it was only a piece of meat that was rotting away.

It was then that the grandfather of a large family died in the village. The lord would be about a hundred years old. They went to see Ogbe-di prepare a coffin for the deceased, to make engravings for him, and to design a sculpture to decorate the grave.

The man who died had been a prestigious priest; all his godchildren, relatives, and the townspeople had a great appreciation for him. The corpse was brought to Ogbe-di's house, even before being brought with Orichaoko.

Ogbe-di spent a few minutes taking some measurements to the man and prepared to work on the coffin. He hired men to do the heavy lifting while he designed and instructed. His assistant, Elegua, assisted him throughout the design and even gave him magnificent ideas. Ogbe-di was very excited about his assistant.

The coffin was a simple matter for Ogbe-di and his workers. The problem was the sculpture. Many ideas came to mind, but he couldn't make up his mind. It took several minutes and, after making some sketches, he put everything aside and went out for air. The sculpture had to express something; It was not just there. And he needed to think clearly.

He tried to rejoin the arduous task of creating the sculpture, but sleep overcame him, and he fell asleep at that long table, next to the older man, who lay motionless, lifeless.

The body was still warm, and it had color; it seemed to be alive. That he only slept.

Ogbe-di would occasionally open her eyes. With his arms resting on the table, his head resting on them, he looked below for a few seconds. Then he closed them again and slept a few more minutes. The sun entered through the entrance of the house and reached his feet. She liked to watch him under the table every time she opened her eyes.

In one of his taps, there was no sun. Ogbe-di was not much surprised; perhaps it is a cloud, he thought. He also felt a breeze, and a chill ran through his arms. He raised his head and looked out. The sun was there, but it did not enter his house. The breeze continued, but not a leaf moved from the trees outside. He stood up and stood at the door, looked inside. The temperature inside her house was cold, unlike the intense heat she felt out. It was clear that something was happening. He felt a presence in his home and could not see it. Therefore, he was sure that it must be related to the mystery of death. Soon the coldness began to stop being felt, and the chills diminished as the sun entered. Ogbe-di remained at the door watching. He was drawn to the shadow on the ground as the sun passed over him. Its shadow reflected the silhouette of a man with wings. The chill returned, and he moved from the place to make sure the shadow was his how light plays with our shadows! He thought. But that situation gave him the idea for the statue. He called his assistant and the workers, and they got to work.

When the family of the deceased went to look for his commission, they were delighted with the design of the coffin. It was a stunning piece. But the statue was rejected at first. When Ogbe-di introduced her, a strange sensation invaded their bodies; It was less than a meter tall. It was awesome. It stood on a block of clay. The sculpture of a man with wings. Or a woman. It was not well distinguished. But it had wings. It was built of clay on black ebony, and the features of the face were not well detailed. The darkness of the room did not reveal the face. It was a beautiful and delicate work, but at the same time chilling. "He is an angel," said Ogbe-di.

Orichaoko and Agana Eri were still in their romance and more and more together. They sold their crops to the sailors in the port, and she helped him with the garden. They had a barge in which they traveled the city through the waters at high tide.

In the port, one day, Orichaoko closed business with some sailors, but the deal did not seem fair to Agana Eri. The fact is that they had too many harvests, and Orichaoko did not want them to spoil. He preferred to sell them at a meager price. Agana disagreed with her husband's decision, and they argued. The discussion became unpleasant, and the sailors walked away, regretting the deal. Orichaoko became even more upset, having lost the business, and he was filled with hatred. His eyes flashed with blood, and his tongue betrayed him.

Damn woman, he said. "So the body is deformed because the gods curse you." The man's words destroyed Agana Eri's heart. Her face was transformed, and her hatred for the man she had once fallen in love with, who had been able to say in public what she had so jealously hidden, was reflected.

He then removed the blanket that covered her, showing her entire twisted body, and her hair turned white. Her eyes widened and angered the entire sea; Going into the waters, he cast a curse on Orichaoko:

"I will hate you for all eternity, and you will live far from me," the enraged witch told her. "And every time I am furious, I will walk through your domain to leave traces of my sadness and disgust, and remind you of the pain you caused me. I will never mention your name again. Everyone who wants to pass through me will pay tribute. And you, Orichaoko, I will punish you with your weapon. Your animals will attack you; your land will become hostile. Your children will not be yours. You will not be able to collect the fruit of your crops, and everyone will step on your land".

The earth began to crack at that moment, and the sea was gathered in a huge wave. The waters attacked the coasts in a single blow, which penetrated the roads and dragged its path with everything it could reach. The houses collapsed, and people ran uselessly because the sea ended up contacting them. So that wave advanced and covered the entire land of the Orichaoko.

Ogbe-di had his house in the mountains of that land, and the water could not reach him there. From the heights, he watched the waters destroy the prosperity of those fertile lands. Many townspeople had time to climb the mountain in search of refuge, but a large crowd of the villagers was devastated by the wrath of Agana Eri.

Elegua, under the guise of an assistant, turned to Ogbe-di and asked him to use his wisdom to end the disaster. But Ogbe-di had no supernatural powers. And he had already distributed all the knowledge on earth. He had kept silence for Olofi to leave him longer, and thus discover what was after death. They all began to implore him to save them. Nerves seized Ogbe-di, and at that moment, he confessed. He no longer had anything to offer.

The water withdrew from the earth, revealing a looted and lifeless terrain; They destroyed crops and the fallen trees. Animals lay on bushes and rocks, and wet bodies. Dying people among the rubble, others trying to survive, and many dead were exposed with the withdrawal of the waters. The houses on the coasts and the ships were merged.

Then the sea was calm again. A few minutes were enough for that destruction to be done. A few minutes were enough to destroy the Orichaoko land.

Orichaoko was washed away by the strong waves and thrown against the trees, the witch took him to the depths, entangled in the water currents, and in a single movement, she left him on the shore, there, in his land, or what was left of that land.

CHAPTER 8
THE COVENANT WITH IKU

Elegua disappeared the moment Ogbe-di had confessed that he had completed his mission on earth. He had also finished his work.

When the worst was over, Ogbe-di and the people who were saved from the terrible event, went down to the city to rescue the survivors, as they walked through the lands and observed the corpses and the great destruction that the sea had left. The feeling of fear is everywhere, and a smell of death that forced to cry. They were able to save a few people. Ogbe-di picked up Orichaoko from the ground and took him home. There he had it, healing the skin and taking care of it, the days I was without knowledge. He left her side and did not leave him for a single moment.

Elegua interceded for Orichaoko against Olofi, but he was too hurt to have hurt Agana Eri.

The medicine and remedies that Ogbe-di used were useless. Orichaoko's body responded favorably for a few minutes and then weakened again. Ogbe-di was fighting something or someone. So the seventh day came, and Ogbe-di began to put candles in the room and some incense sticks. He covered the body with flowers. The only flowers that had survived the disaster, because they were on top of the mountain. He prepared some seeds and hung them all over the room. He knew he was not doing his job in vain. He had already gone too far, and Orichaoko was still alive.

He began to pray, hoping he could save Orichaoko. He spent the whole day praying. On knees. For a moment, he thought that it was right there where the man who had made the coffin was.

Orichaoko was well-loved in that land and the only one who could recover it from the devastation. With Olofi on his back, no deity wanted to intervene.

The whole day passed, and Ogbe-di received no answer to his prayers, and suddenly Orichaoko's body began to tremble. The temperature started to rise, and the Orichaoko's body was not responding to the treatment that Ogbe-di applied. He put pressure on his chest because his body seemed to be falling off the table. White foam came out of his mouth, and his eyes widened and ran behind. Orichaoko's black complexion began to show a whitish tint, and that deep, weakened breath returned and expelled the air. That last breath that set the soul free. I've seen it before, in the man in the red hat. The body stopped shaking. It went out, gently, until it was completely relaxed, and that's when the breeze blew again, and the candles suddenly went out, and the sun went down like that time, it only shone outside. But now, when Ogbe-di looked at the door, the silhouette of a tall woman was covering the sun. He had a sickle in his hands, a small sickle that moves from side to side.

He entered the house, and Ogbe-di couldn't even blink. He stared at the woman who covered the sun as she approached Orichaoko's body with a smooth movement. Her gray hair floated in that room as if it lacked an atmosphere.

Everything around him was paralyzed; As if time doesn't mean anything at the moment. The long dress did not show the feet, but due to the way she moved, she did not have it either; A Piercing, dark gaze on that colorless face.

I had never seen Ogbe-di before a white woman. Not so silky hair. The fine silks caressing the body of the flying woman did not look like dresses. They were like fabrics harmoniously arranged on his skin, without motives or particular works; She just glided smoothly and delicately over her firm breasts. Ogbe-di could feel fear and silence. Like a ringing in the ear that muffled any sound in the room. But no one else could perceive that presence. It was as if they were there but in another dimension.

You get to see the wind and the particles that are reflected through the sun. And he also saw how, with his brilliant sickle, he hooked Orichaoko's soul. The transparent and inert spirit of the farmer and owner of these lands followed the woman, so if you can leave in peace! Ogbe-di considered. It was a good company for a trip of that magnitude.

That is why the face of the man in the red hat was full of peace when he was leaving the earth. There was no doubt that this impressive and mysterious creature had come looking for him.

"Stop, you can't take it with you!" Ogbe-di's rumbling scream broke the silence of the room and made the woman turn her gaze to him. The woman's face that reflects peace now expressed her amazement.

"Can you see me?" She asked. Her voice was delicate like the silks that covered her. "How is it possible?".

In a quick and surprising movement, she approached Ogbe-di and sniffed him as if trying to identify if he was alive. Even his amazement impressed her. He knew of people who saw spirits in the graveyards. And of some who could communicate with the souls of the dead. But I had never known a living being that could see death.

"Why can't I take it with me? He already belongs to me!" She said, very sure. "There is nothing you can do for him!"

"I am Ogbe-di, the wisest man on earth."

She was staring at him in amazement and eager to understand why he could see her. What was unique about this man who was able to see death and speak to him?

"I can offer you a lot in exchange for Orichaoko's life and the salvation of this town. I offer you my wisdom. And that's all the knowledge in the world! Doesn't the proposal appeal to you?" Said Ogbe-di.

Death relaxing, he leaned back and, after a brief pause, asked him: "Do you know everything?"

"Yes, all the secrets that Olofi sent to earth," he replied.

"Then explain to me how you can see me," said the restless death.

"I have all the answers because I have all the knowledge. The only thing I don't know is what exists beyond death. Accept my proposal, and you will have your answer," confessed Ogbe-di.

"Let's make a pact," death said to Ogbe-di, smiling and curious.

"I bring Orichaoko back to life; in short, I don't need it. In return, you give me all your wisdom. But I can't answer your question," death told him with a grimace of arrogance and self-sufficiency.

"The answer to that question is so great that it does not fit in the knowledge. Olofi was unable to send that secret to earth. Something sacred and mysterious that crosses cultures and dimensions; it is not about spirit or religion, it is not expressed in words; Only those who visit my domains can know what is there, and it is not allowed to carry the body, and souls do not usually return."

Ogbe-di's words of death had become clear to him. The floating woman had shattered his dreams with his words. Now I felt emptiness and need. Curiosity disarmed him in doubt.

"What if you send me back to earth?" He asked her, "And what would you give me in return? If you gave me the knowledge in exchange for Orichaoko's life, you would have nothing more to offer." said the cunning death.

"I still have something that may interest you. I know that you have always wanted to come to the world of the living and be able to be together with the men of the earth in the same dimension. I can give you the name of the person who has that power. " Iku kept analyzing Ogbe-di's proposal.

After a brief pause, she decided to seal the pact with the wise man.

With the sickle, she cut a deep cut in the palm of her hand, and, when Ogbe-di's blood fell on the ground, in a whirlwind of wind, she released Orichaoko's soul and hooked Ogbe-di's. He made that quick move back to the door, and Ogbe-di's soul turned to look back as he headed off to death.

The wise man watched his lifeless body gently collapse. It was strange, but he didn't feel like it belonged to him. He looked around the room and could see how Orichaoko took a deep breath and released it with a dry, suffocating cough with pain. Recovering the soul hurts, was the last thought of Ogbe-di, as his spirit left towards the answer to his only doubt. As it moved away, the soul could hear, see, smell, all the senses functioned as if it still used its body.

He tried to see himself, but there was nothing there; he imagined his arms and legs, but none of that existed; His soul was not even smoke.

Soon her soul disappeared with the beautiful death, and time and movement returned to Ogbe-di's house. Orichaoko coughed until his breathing returned to normal. Those with him helped him up and realized that Ogbe-di was lying on the ground. Dead.

CHAPTER 9
THE RETURN OF OGBE-DI

Death gained all the knowledge, and with it, the answer to her questions. She also had the name of who would assist her in her plans to cross into the world of the living. And several years had passed since she had taken Ogbe-di to know his secrets. It was time to fulfill his part of the covenant and return him to earth.

After Ogbe-di's death, all people followed his teachings.

Orichaoko and the survivors of the land, after months of drought, managed to make the gods bless them and save the earth.

A rain of seven days in a row made the ground wet again, and the crops that had not been grown for a long time grew; And the place came alive. They repaired the temple in the name of Ogbe-di, the temple that he built on the mountain. Inside it had thick columns, and a corridor lit by candles and oil lamps, and outside, the rough walls supported a glossy dome that protruded and was visible throughout the city.

They were all on their knees, arms raised,

praying to the gods in one voice as he walked the halls of his temple. Ogbe-di did not know any of those faces, but he knew their names, their lives. He knew his children, their sorrows, their fears, the darkest secrets, just by looking at them. I knew their destinations. I knew their deaths. And where would they go next? Now he did know everything.

He left the temple and decided to go down to the town in search of a familiar face. Everything had changed. In the city, they built walls and canals to protect themselves from floods. The houses had been repaired, and the floors were fertile. Through one of the fields, he saw a cart approach with two oxen. And that umbrella that he had made with his own hands.

Orichaoko came with his oxen and passed him by the side while Ogbe-di greeted him. He didn't recognize him, he thought. And he ran after the oxen for a long time while calling him.

Why wouldn't Orichaoko want to stop? The cart was on its way to the temple. Ogbe-di followed the path uphill back to the temple. And when they arrived, they were all outside looking at the sun. He spoke to them, touched them, shook them; they turned around, they looked but ignored him. He stood behind them and began to talk.

"Hey, it's me!" He said. "I came back from death." But nobody listened to him; They kept praying, looking at the sky and surrounding the large ceiba tree. Ogbe-di began to tell where he had gone. He started talking to them about death. What is it, where is it, what is that place like? People still ignored him, but as the man who knew everything spoke, satisfaction appeared on his face; The pleasure of having achieved everything he wanted. He was more satisfied because he had outwitted Olofi and death.

As he recounted his experience with death, people turned to him. Downcast and walking forward. Towards the road, towards the town. Ogbe-di thought they had turned to look at him. To listen to it, as they always did. What had changed? Didn't they believe him anymore? What ungrateful people! He had sacrificed everything for them, and now they ignored it. Little by little, one after another, they withdrew from that place. Ogbe-di went to the tree. There was something there that caused him doubt. Something that wasn't there before. That it wasn't when he lived there, as he got closer he looked around: The people were gone. Ogbe-di was left alone in that place. Alone, under the huge ceiba tree. Alone, and staring at a beautiful angel adorning a gravestone engraved with his name.

OGBE-DI
YOUR KNOWLEDGE IS SHARED
BETWEEN PEOPLE

Raul Dominguez

Cuban writer, born on November 22, 1981, in Havana, Cuba. He traveled to the united states, where he has developed his works.

Author of several educational documents, related to Afro-Cuban culture and Yoruba religion. He promotes conscious, logical reasoning, and rescue ancient customs and forgotten rituals.

Recognized Orihate of the Yoruba religious cultural society of Cuba, distinguished for his investigation of all history related to Afro-Cuban religious culture.

"Ogbe-di (8-7) is a sign of the oracle of Ifa. There are 256 signs, and they all leave us teachings and tell stories. In this novel, I wanted to incarnate Ogbe-di to carry a message beyond the religious. And I adapted my work so that it would be appreciated by all people regardless of their creed."

www.ingramcontent.com/pod-product-compliance
Lightning Source LLC
Chambersburg PA
CBHW071512150726
48000CB00002B/545